LOOKING BACK

For Margaret,
Ruth, Frances, Denis, Hugh,
Brian Walker, Neil Shawcross, William Johnston, Jim Bennett
— encouragers all — with my thanks

The Friar's Bush Press
24 College Park Avenue
Belfast BT7 1LR
Published 1989
© Copyright reserved
ISBN 0 946872 25 2

Designed by Rodney Miller Associates, Belfast.
Printed by W. & G. Baird, Antrim.

Photographs by Arthur Campbell 1939-60

Friar's Bush Press

INTRODUCTION

Arthur Campbell, 1948

My first book of photographs, *Return journey* ended at the outbreak of war in 1939. In *Looking back* the photographs cover the period 1939—60 and are divided into sections dealing with Dublin, Belfast and my artist friends.

When news of the start of war broke I went down to a photographic shop in High Street and bought all the 3×4 centimetre film that was in stock. For the next five years, however, because of wartime censorship I photographed very little in Belfast. Instead, cheap day excursions and weekends staying at the youth hostel in Mountjoy Square, allowed me to photograph interesting parts of the city of Dublin.

In spite of wartime restrictions, my brother George and I, with members of our circle of friends, Gerard Dillon, Daniel O'Neill, Olive Henry, James MacIntyre and Thomas McCreanor, when we had a little money, went to the Mournes and the Antrim Coast and painted landscapes or seascapes.

With the lifting of restrictions after the end of the war I returned to photographing Belfast. Seen today, the photographs capture a city and people reviving after the war and the blitz which had so devastated parts of Belfast.

Some photographs fleshed out five-minute sketches and colour notes when I painted at home; five minutes on a pen drawing because I could not ask my companions to wait while I spent time on details. In any event a black cloud meant that soon the rain would put a halt to my gallop.

The camera was a surrogate drawing pad, which explains why some photographs have affinities with certain paintings. Sketches were made to be brought home and studied to form the basis of pictures but often there were aspects which were not paintworthy; or there was not time, to say nothing of my ability to record them. It was then the camera came into its own.

Arthur Campbell October 1989

DUBLIN

Nelson Pillar in O'Connell Street, Dublin, seen from the General Post Office. An explosion felled the Pillar on 8th March 1966.

16 May 1937

Kerbside fruit offered on crates and on a typical Dublin three-wheeler where Marlborough Street joined Earl Street, not far from Nelson Pillar.

23 October 1948

2

"Bicycle Parks" took the place of petrol-starved cars in O'Connell Street, Dublin, during "The Emergency" of 1939—45. As a neutral country, the lights stayed on and a trip to Dublin from a blacked-out north of Ireland took one into an illuminated grotto. The cinema is presenting "Hello Frisco Hello" and tramcars continued to travel on both sides of the wide tree-lined thoroughfare. Horse-cabs came out of retirement and were useful, provided there was no hurry.

17 August 1943

Petrol was available only for vital services and taxis between 1939 and
1945. The all-day parking fee for a bicycle was six pence.
O'Connell Street, Dublin.

                    17 August 1943

Cathal Brugha Street, off O'Connell Street, Dublin, and St Thomas's
Church.

7 April 1953

5

The advance guard, on Easter Sunday 1953, of the parade which
marked the inauguration of the *An Tostal* festivals throughout the
country. It is passing Elvery's *Elephant House* in O'Connell Street. The
photograph was taken from the editorial office of *The Bell* monthly
journal.

5 April 1953

The centrepiece of the nation-wide *An Tostal* celebrations was a bowl with a continuously burning flame on O'Connell Bridge, Dublin, in a specially constructed flower garden. Trinity College and the Bank of Ireland are visible at the end of Westmoreland Street, in College Green.

8 April 1953

There was continuous banter between stallholders and shoppers in
Moore Street, Dublin. A friend of mine reported back to Belfast that he
heard a trader crying her wares with "Fine ripe Jaffas and Seville
oranges! None of your foreign trash sold here."

23 October 1948

Typical Dublin wicker baskets on three wheels, which carried goods "through streets broad and narrow" to kerbside markets and stalls. Sometimes they had plank sides instead of wicker, or prams were used. To me, they are peculiar to Dublin.

circa 1946

My brother George Campbell took me on a walkabout to places which had caught his fancy in the twelve months since his going to live in Dublin. We made sketches: George for his large painting *Dublin*; I with a watercolour in mind. We paused at the second-hand books displayed at the Eden Quay corner of O'Connell Bridge and I make a hasty drawing of the cart of books at 2d. each, to be fleshed out later with help of my photograph when I painted the scene in watercolour.

23 October 1948

The "Tuppenny Barrow," Eden Quay, Dublin.

23 October 1948

11

Burgh Quay and O'Connell Bridge.

1946

The Abbey Theatre, Dublin, which was destroyed by fire in July 1951.

21 August 1943

The Ha'penny Bridge over the River Liffey in Dublin, seen from Merchant's Arch on the quay. I can just remember when there was a turnstile at either end of the bridge and my mother let me pay the toll. That must have been about 1918, or earlier. Was the toll a ha'penny?

30 August 1946

14

Fruit-sellers at the Ha'penny Bridge where it meets Bachelor's Walk.
30 August 1946

15

The makers of Pentax cameras have an exhibition gallery in London for photographs. This one of the view, into Liffey Street, Dublin, from the Ha'penny Bridge, was chosen for display and Pentax said "it has captured some of the atmosphere of earlier times."

30 August 1946

16

I remembered in the 'Twenties seeing a life-sized wooden horse and a man ringing a bell outside an auction room in Bachelor's Walk, Dublin. By 1948, they had gone but I took this photograph for old time's sake and because the ornamental ironwork pleased me. The railings were at

J. P. Cahill and Company, not far from O'Connell Bridge.

23 October 1948

Merchant's Arch and Commercial Court seen from the
Ha'penny Bridge, Dublin.

21 August 1943

Looking out of Commercial Court and Merchant's Arch to
Bachelor's Walk on the opposite side of the River Liffey,
Dublin.

21 August 1946

19

Barrel-laden Guinness steam lighters began operations on Dublin's River Liffey in 1873 and were taken out of commission in 1961. Small boys hung over the bridges to wait for the 'captain' to fold the funnel down in order to clear a low arch; then, if their aim was good, they spat straight into the furnace. Here, one of the vessels is passing the Four Courts on its up-river return trip from Custom House Quay to the brewery.

27 February 1951

A Guinness lighter with "empties" steaming up-river to the brewery at
St James's Gate.

27 February 1951

The Brazen Head in Bridge Street is the oldest public house in Dublin, going back to before 1688. It was a stopping-place for horse-drawn coaches and I saw a row of narrow bedrooms upstairs on my first visit in 1946. Oliver Bond, one of the planners of the 1798 Rising, lived at No. 13 Bridge Street, and the Brazen Head was a meeting-place for the conspirators. The shops seen here in the foreground have since been demolished.

25 August 1955

The Brazen Head, Bridge Street, Dublin.

25 August 1955

23

A gateway in Back Lane, Dublin, caught my brother George's fancy. He thought it might have an association with the "Back Lane Parliament" of Wolfe Tone's time. He made a drawing and asked me to record the ironwork. Tone spoke often in the Tailor's Hall which was derelict in the early 'fifties. It was close to us but the angle of view was too narrow to take a satisfactory photograph.

24 February 1951

24

Thomas Moore was born in 1779 at 12 Aungier Street, Dublin. His "Irish Melodies" drew largely on the airs taken by Edward Bunting in Belfast. Although a legend and bust on the exterior extol the poet, there was nothing inside the public house in the way of relics of Moore.

24 June 1955

25

The Busaras, or Aras Mhic Dhiarmada (MacDermott Building) was opened as the central bus station in Store Street, Dublin, a short while before I took this photograph.

28 October 1954

26

The waiting area at the Busaras, the central bus station,
Dublin. The racing news helped to while away the time.
28 October 1954

27

The Presbyterian Association's building seen from St Stephen's Green, Dublin.

11 October 1947

Huband Bridge (1791) on the Grand Canal, Dublin.
29 August 1946

29

I wanted a record of St Audoen's Church, the oldest church in Dublin, as seen from the rear. The church was founded by the Anglo-Normans in the thirteenth century. The caravans in the foreground were in Cook Street, one of the most historic streets in old Dublin, which can be traced by name back to 1270, and is referred to as the Vicus Cocorum in old documents, because the medieval guild of cooks were once centred there. The caravans were sited beneath a length of the ancient city walls. I got my photograph of St. Audoen's, too.

27 February 1951

A cab waiting for passengers coming off a train at Harcourt Street
station, Dublin, the terminus of the Dublin South Eastern Railway. The
last train left the station for Bray, Co. Wicklow on 31st December 1958.

26 August 1942

More than a year after the end of hostilities (in 1945), there was still
universal dependence on wood and peat. Here, a turf-barge is
unloading beside Leeson Street bridge on the Grand Canal, Dublin.

29 August 1946

At Lansdowne Road ground in Dublin, before the International Rugby
match between Ireland and France.

29 January 1949

33

BELFAST

The Crown Saloon faces across Great Victoria Street in Belfast to the Europa Hotel and the Grand Opera House. This photograph was taken from the Great Northern Railway's station complex which occupied the site of the present-day hotel. The Crown was taken over by the National Trust towards the end of the seventies and refurbished after much of its exterior tilework and stained glass was damaged by a bomb blast. Fortunately, the original moulds were found and used to make new tiles. C. E. B. Brett, in his monumental *Buildings of Belfast* calls the Crown ". . . an example of the very richest and most mellow period of pub architecture . . . one of the finest High Victorian buildings in Belfast . . . it seems to date from about 1885."

27 June 1953

The Thompson Memorial Fountain (1885) has as part of its inscription "Whoso drinketh of the water that I shall give him . . .". The fountain has been dry for many years. The BBC building is close to the fountain in Ormeau Avenue, Belfast.

14 May 1948

An overcoat cost fifty shillings in Magee's of Royal Avenue, Belfast, in 1905. That was no bargain, really, for in 1946 the Two Ten Tailors of North Street pictured here, were offering a suit — jacket, trousers and waistcoat — for fifty shillings and there was no extra charge for altering the turn-ups to make the trousers the correct length. The flower-seller's customer is carrying a bunch of daffodils bought for sixpence.

6 April 1946

For some years after Belfast was bombed in 1941, a large space in High Street attracted a multitude of open-air sellers of knick-knacks. I made a pencil drawing of a man offering daffodils and thought a tramcar would make a background, so this photograph was to remind me of details when I painted a watercolour at home. River House stands there now.

6 April 1946

37

The area to the west of St Anne's Cathedral in Belfast was being changed when I took this photograph from a bus halted by traffic. The ground left flat when the International Bar was destroyed by the 1941 air raids became a market-place for street traders. A Dutch auction was being held at the back of a motor truck. I remember that the International's rubble was still smouldering a month after the incendiaries fell.

27 April 1957

The west side of Bridge Street, Belfast, being re-built on ground which
had been undeveloped since the 1941 blitz: the two aerial attacks that
left 1,500 dead and vast destruction. The donkey was making its way
along High Street towards Castle Place.

17 June 1959

The Harry Ferguson building in Donegall Square East, Belfast, was for many years the showpiece and centre for Austin cars. The company was the sole distributor of Austin cars and commercial vehicles and had a network of franchised agents throughout the province. Harry Ferguson was chairman of the company and in 1946 wished to meet his recently appointed publicity manager: me. I had to plead that I could not follow his description of the farm tractor he would unveil later that year. I insisted that I knew nothing about engineering or farming, though I could put words together, take a photograph, or draft a newspaper story or an advertisement. He conceded "Quite right, Mr Campbell. We invited you to manage our publicity, not for your engineering experience. I hope you will be successful in telling farmers and motorists what we sell."

6 May 1948

A display in a rear window of the Harry Ferguson building in Upper Arthur Street, Belfast. The theme was "Go Places with Austin." The Ferguson company was the distributor of Austin cars for Northern Ireland. It was in the attic space of this building that Harry Ferguson did the experimental work that led to his famous tractor.

Spring, 1946

The platform of a parked lorry gave a better perspective for a photograph than one taken from ground level and lessened the problem of sloping verticals. The Samuel McCausland company left Victoria Street in Belfast for Mallusk, a few miles to the north of the city, in the 1970s but the mouldings will still have a place in the vast re-development area bounded by Queen's Square, Donegall Quay, Ann Street and Victoria Street. McCausland's took over its next door neighbour and chief competitor in the seed business, in 1959.

2 May 1953

The Samuel McCausland building in Victoria Street, Belfast.
4 December 1950

The steel forest of gantries and cranes in Harland and Wolff's Queen's
Island shipyard in Belfast has gone, and instead, *Goliath* and *Samson*,
two towering yellow structures, can be seen from far away.

15 June 1957

44

I "stole" this photograph, from my seat in the Empire Theatre, Belfast, on the first night of Sam Thompson's *Over the Bridge.* Left to right on stage are Roy Alcorn, J. G. Devlin (seated behind Alcorn), Joseph Tomelty, Sam Thompson (seated) and Harry Towb.

29 January 1960

45

Arthur Cahoon's Hairdressing Saloon was at XXXII Donegall Road,
Belfast, beside McFarland's Court.

9 September 1950

McFarland's Court was a short distance from Shaftesbury Square, Belfast. The lady on the left started to rise from her box when I began to focus my camera.

9 September 1950

47

Hamilton's butcher's shop at 189 Lisburn Road, Belfast, was cheek by jowl with the barber's saloon at the corner of Donnybrook Street.

5 July 1956

48

My memory of the man with the trumpet is of hearing a
line or two of a hymn before he proffered his hat, then
moved on a few paces and repeated the same hymn.
Outside the Mol Gallery in Queen Street, Belfast.

4 March 1944

Horse-drawn milk floats were being seen less often in 1960. Motor transport took over and nudged horses off the streets while tractors took over on farms. The scene is Botanic Avenue, Belfast.

9 October 1960

50

"Wee Willie Winkie" Campbell was a well-loved Belfast character. He was for a long time stationed outside Robinson Cleavers, playing his saw with a violin bow. The annual agricultural show with its crowds took him to the south of the city and it was outside the Royal Ulster showgrounds at Balmoral that I spotted him.

26 May 1955

Chipperfield's circus in Ormeau Park, Belfast.

27 June 1959

The giraffe in Chipperfield's circus in Ormeau Park,
Belfast, was a favourite with children.

27 June 1959

June is when the great pyres begin to build up in Belfast's side streets. As the Orangemen's day on the Twelfth of July comes close, children beg, borrow and collect, piles of combustibles such as tyres, tea chests, old sofas, worm-ridden furniture and, if the ganger is unsighted, the tree stumps from building sites. "Aye, it is terrible heavy but it rolls if we all push at the same time. It's for the stack of ould boxes we've gathered for the Twalfth bonefire. Will ye take wer photo, mister? Hi, Billy, Alec, all of youse, he's going to take wer picture. Get your han's on an' shove!" The bonfires blaze from the night before until well into the small hours of the Twelfth of July.

7 May 1960

The boys were in the top saloon of a tramcar on Shankill
Road, Belfast. I am not sure if the ha'penny fare and a
blue ticket for children up to 14 years of age still applied.
The inscription reads "Please retain your tickets for
inspection."

17 July 1951

The 'gothic' arch, where Greencastle left off and Whitehouse began, led to a sunken square of cottages and the view was towards Belfast Lough and passing vessels. I painted two versions, each with children to enliven the scene, and one is in the Ulster Museum and Art Gallery, Belfast.

11 October 1956

56

The shore of Belfast Lough at Whitehouse was a place to find small crabs. They were put into tin cans and tipped out when it was time for the boys to go home.

8 September 1956

ARTISTS

Olive Henry, a designer of stained glass by profession, is a considerable artist. She with Richard Faulkner, a fellow member of the Royal Ulster Academy, and myself founded the art group of the Youth Hostel Association in the late 1930s. One rendezvous was near Bloody Bridge hostel between Newcastle and Annalong. The photograph shows Olive busy and unaware.

25 February 1940

Myself above the sea-cleft and pool, Breaghy cliffs,
Portnablagh, Donegal.

31 July 1945

Theo Gracey did much painting in Antrim and Donegal. His car was a
shelter on a cold, wet day at Whitepark Bay, north Antrim, when
outdoor painting was impossible. He was a noted calligrapher as well
as a landscape painter. Theo Gracey exhibited in Belfast and Dublin
and was a Royal Ulster Academician.

16 February 1941

Theo Gracey at Brackenagh near Kilkeel, County Down. The mist
advancing down the Mourne Mountains flank blanketed all detail and
we beat a retreat.

25 February 1940

One of my many affectionate memories of Maurice Wilks and his wife
Berry is of his leaving the cottage at Brablagh, Cushendun, and
bringing home the lythe he had caught, long before I was awake.

19 September 1943

Maurice Wilks in his studio at Cushendun on the Antrim coast. He ranged widely for his landscapes — Kerry, Donegal, the west of Ireland, Antrim — and painted some portraits during the war years at the request of servicemen stationed in Northern Ireland. He was an Associate Academician of the Royal Hibernian Academy, and a popular member of the Youth Hostel art group.
30 April 1944

I was one of a party which boarded a train in Bloomfield station, east Belfast, in the war-time summer of 1942. Facing me was William Conor, whom I had long known, by his pork-pie hat and bow tie, to be the artist who painted Belfast people from behind an opened newspaper. He was interested in where we were going — the Mournes — and was told we would walk from Newcastle to a youth hostel with our rucksacks which held our needs for the week-end. The suburban railway station was in use because an Army bomb-disposal unit was working to unearth an unexploded aerial torpedo which had been buried beside the track at Connswater since the air raids of the previous year. William Conor and his fellow traveller, Mrs Allen, alighted at Comber, just as I was hoping to steal another picture.

20 June 1942

Daniel O'Neill's paintings are highly regarded now but were not to the taste of the Belfast galleries whose interest lay in glass and china and in art materials rather than art. His death in 1974 brought a tribute from friends, extracts from which read: "Dan should have been born at the turn of the century . . . he would undoubtedly have searched out Vlaminck, Utrillo, and Modigliani . . . he wore a cape for a while and in those days, when artists were suspect, it was quite a gesture but he fitted the part and knew it." O'Neill's paintings are in important public and private collections in Ireland, Britain, the U.S.A., Australia, and New Zealand. He was sitting at the famous "Table at the Window" in the restaurant facing across Donegall Square to the City Hall during a break from an exhibition in Donegall Place.

circa 1948

George Campbell and I presented an exhibition of paintings and drawings in the Mol Gallery, Queen Street, Belfast. It was George's first time to exhibit, apart from some black-and-white work in the Gaelic League's Golden Jubilee show in St Mary's Hall, Bank Street, Belfast, of 1943. He hung many drawings of United States servicemen and some of his experiences in the 1941 bombings and we were pleased that twenty-eight pictures were bought and with the good reports in the Press. (Photograph by the late J. Bonar Holmes)

28 February 1944

At the two-man Campbell exhibition in the Mol Gallery, Queen Street, Belfast. From the left: George Campbell, John Mol, Theo Gracey, and Arthur Campbell. (Photograph by the late J. Bonar Holmes)

28 February 1944

One wall in Mol's Gallery was given over to my watercolours of the Mourne area, County Antrim, and Kerry. I hung some black-and-white drawings too, but they clashed with the paintings and were taken away. (Photograph by the late J. Bonar Holmes)

28 February 1944

At the opening of an exhibition by Gerard Dillon and George Campbell in the Lamb Gallery in Portadown, 1944, John Hewitt (with pipe) poet and keeper of art at Belfast Municipal Art Gallery and Museum (now the Ulster Museum) and T. G. F. Patterson, Curator of Armagh County Museum. Arthur Lamb had a decorating business and set aside a room for his brother Charles's paintings, made largely from his base at Carraroe, County Galway. Arthur Lamb's sisters bought a picture from Gerard and from George — the only ones sold during the exhibition — and I was invited to join them for a meal in the hospitable Lamb home.

26 June 1944

Grouped before the paintings by Dillon and Campbell in Arthur
Lamb's short-lived gallery in Portadown were from left, Mark
Saunders, an artist serving in the Royal Canadian Air Force, Patricia
Webb, Arthur Lamb, Maimie Grey, Gerard Dillon and George
Campbell.

26 June 1944

Paul Nietsche's one-man exhibition in the CEMA gallery, Donegall
Place, Belfast. CEMA (Council for the Encouragement of Music and the
Arts) was the forerunner of the Arts Council of Northern Ireland.
From the left: Roberta Hewitt, Nietsche and John Hewitt.

May 1948

Markey Robinson (seated) wished to have a record of his
large oil painting in McDowall's public house on Shankill
Road, Belfast, and asked me to take a photograph.

25 June 1945

72

Interior of McDowall's on Shankill Road, Belfast.

25 June 1945

Artist James MacIntyre at work in Falls Park, west Belfast.
4 October 1947

74

Arthur Armstrong in Falls Park, west Belfast.

4 October 1947

Zoltan lewinter-Frankl had the most important collection of paintings owned privately in Northern Ireland. Here he is, on the left, greeting a visitor to the Victor Waddington Gallery, South Anne Street, Dublin, at the opening of the one-man exhibition of Philip Moysey's pictures. In centre: the Chevalier Thomas MacGreevy, poet and director of the National Gallery and on the right, Rev. Father Senan, D.F.M., Cap.

8 June 1950

Zoltan lewinter-Frankl (on left) with Oskar Kokoschka at
the exhibition of Philip Moysey's pictures: Victor
Waddington Gallery, Dublin.

8 June 1950

George Campbell, Sir John Keane, and (on right) George Waddington, in the Victor Waddington Gallery, South Anne Street, Dublin. The gallery was presenting a one-man Campbell exhibition.

22 May 1951

I had admired the few of Nano Reid's paintings I had
seen previously on visits to Dublin so I enjoyed what I
saw in her studio in No. 1 Fitzwilliam Square, Dublin.
25 August 1946

79

My mother, Gretta Bowen's "Pilgrimage" oil painting: an example of how her naive imagination made use of memory, however tenuous, to portray boats and pilgrims nearing the Basilica on Lough Derg. She had no artistic training and did not begin to create her lively paintings until she was 70. She died in 1981.

4 February 1957